to Children at Waterloo Elem.

MARILEE ROBIN BURTON

My Best Shoes

PAINTINGS BY JAMES E. RANSOME

"   .   7   .   98

James Ransome

Keep Reading!

TAMBOURINE BOOKS   NEW YORK

Text copyright © 1994 by Marilee Robin Burton

Illustrations copyright © 1994 by James E. Ransome

Printed in the United States of America

Library of Congress Cataloging in Publication Data

Burton, Marilee R. My best shoes/by Marilee R. Burton; illustrated by James E. Ransome. —1st ed. p. cm.
Summary: Celebrates the variety of shoes that can be worn, from sturdy lace up high shoes to naked feet and toe shoes.
[1. Shoes—Fiction. 2. Stories in rhyme.] I. Ransome, James E., ill. II. Title. PZ8.3.B969My 1994 [E]—dc20 92-33863 CIP AC
ISBN 0-688-11756-2 (trade)   ISBN 0-688-11757- 0 (lib.bdg.)
10 9 8 7 6 5 4 3 2 1
First edition

*For Sara J. Rodriguez, who almost always
wears sneakers (never tennis shoes)*   M.R.B.

To Charlie Bogasat, teacher and friend   J.E.R.

On Monday I wore tie shoes
Sturdy lace up high shoes
Tie them in a bow shoes
Knot them in a tangle shoes

Oops...don't let them dangle shoes.

On Tuesday I wore tap shoes

Buckle and strap shoes
With one little snap shoes
Learn how to dance shoes
Twirl and prance shoes.

On Wednesday I wore play shoes
Gray shoes
Run all day shoes
Race, skip, and hop shoes

Jump and then stop shoes.

On Thursday I wore old shoes

Dirty brown and gold shoes
Scratched and scuffed and muffed shoes
Scruffed shoes
Not polished or buffed shoes.

On Friday I wore new shoes
Bright and shiny blue shoes
Twinkling in the light shoes
Sparkling in the night shoes

What a pretty sight shoes!

On Saturday I wore sun shoes

Just for fun shoes
Tiptoe in the sand shoes
Water, grass, and land shoes
Carry in my hand shoes.

On Sunday I wore no shoes
Naked feet and toe shoes
Barefoot all day long shoes
Sing a summer song shoes
Can't go wrong shoes....

They're my very best!